Feeling Christmas

Written by Mandy Bare

Illustrated by Izzi Ciesinska and William Day

For Isabella Rosalee, Christmas was
the best time of the year.

Christmas gave her a feeling that
she couldn't figure out!
It was a feeling of mushiness, a
feeling of gushiness,
squishiness and joy that made
her heart feel warm
like the

Sunshine.

Her excitement bubbled
as her *happiness* doubled,
until she had to jump up and down
and twirl all around!

And her heart was filled with

Love.

So much love that she wanted to hug!

But the feeling was also **calm**
Like listening to soft music
and staring up at the
sparkling
lights.

Now WHERE this feeling was coming from
is what she couldn't figure out!
She had been thinking about it a lot,
and this feeling,
she was sure,
wasn't from
a bag
or a box
or a store.

So she hopped on
The Polar Express
and set off to the North Pole,
determined to figure out where this
mushy, gushy, squishy-wishy, sunshine-happy
feeling was
coming from.

Wow! She always imagined The North Pole
would be magical,
but this was absolutely positively majestically

fantastical.

How exciting it was when the elves
let her help
cling clang and **bing bang**
the toys into perfection.

She stared at these amazing toys
and wondered to herself,
"Could toys be where this happy
and exciting,
yet calm and enlightening
feeling was coming from?"

She thought and she thought.
She felt and she felt.
"Hmmm. . . no it had not."

She knew there was something very
special about this
Christmas Season
but she was having trouble finding
the reason.

Then amazement filled her eyes
as she began to realize
that the soft, red belly
she had just bumped into
belonged to
Santa Claus!

"Ho! Ho! Ho!" he said
with a wink and a smile.

He sat down in his chair
and put Isabella on his knee.
She told him that she had been
a **good** girl and all,
so he reached in his sack
and pulled out a doll.

It was the bestest-ever doll
that she always wanted,
that can walk and talk
and giggle and wiggle!

Santa and presents must be it!
The feeling must come from him.
She thought and she thought.
She felt and she felt.
"Hmmm. . . it is so exciting
to see Santa and get presents,
but this feeling I'm feeling
of Christmas
it isn't."

And oh what joy when Rudolph said,
"Hop on!
Let's go for a ride!"
They *whizzed* and they whirled.
They spinned and they *twirled*.
The stars glittered and twinkled
and sparkled and sprinkled.

She wondered if
Rudolph brought the
fantastically-fabulous, absolutely *delicious*
feeling of Christmas.

She thought and she thought.
She felt and she felt.
"I love **Rudolph**
and having fun for sure,
but something tells me
this feeling is
much
much more."

She now knew
the feeling didn't come from the
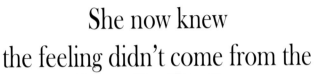
so she politely asked
her **red**-nosed friend
to drop her off
at her home again.

She had arrived just in time
to go Christmas caroling
with her family.
As they walked past the church
she was **drawn** to the manger scene
with Joseph, Mary, and baby Jesus.

She felt something warm
that started in her HEART.
Then it spread out
and grew
until it turned into joy.
It was mushy and gushy,
and *peaceful* and calm.
She felt SO happy and excited that
she wanted to hug,
and she wanted to love.

With the feelings of Christmas
all rolled into one,
she could finally see where they all had come from!

So excitedly she exclaimed, "I found it! I found it!
This is what Christmas is really about!"

She ran over to
the baby
and stared down at His
sweet face.
"It's Jesus, Mom. It's Jesus."

What is the spirit we feel at Christmastime?
It is His Spirit – the Spirit of Christ.

He gave us His service, His love and His life.

"Merry Christmas!"